How Fox Became Red

A Folktale from the Athabaskan Indians of Alaska
to Read and Tell

Retold by Martha Hamilton and Mitch
Beauty and the Beast Storytellers

Illustrated by Kathy O'Malley

D1306145

 Richard C. Owen Publishers, Inc.
Katonah, New York

Fox didn't always have beautiful red fur.
Long ago his fur was a dull shade of gray.

But one day that changed, and here
is how it happened.

3

While Fox was out hunting, he saw a whole family of geese at the edge of the lake.

"Mmm," Fox thought,
"Those geese look delicious. What a
tasty meal they would make!"

5

Fox bounded toward the geese.
He was so hungry and so excited
about eating them that he began
to sing, "Geese meat! Geese meat!
Mmm, mmm, mmm!"

When the geese heard Fox's song,
they rushed to the water.
They jumped in and swam far away
until they were in the middle of the lake.

Fox ran around the lake, snapping
and snarling at the geese.

He grew angrier and angrier.

Fox was in such a rage that his dull gray fur
turned bright red.

Fox has remained red to this day because
he is still so mad about not eating those geese.